Englische Fußballgeschichten | Spannende Fußballgeschichten für spielerisches Lernen | Mit Vokabeln, Grammatik, interaktiven Übungen, lustigen Quiz und Audio-Unterstützung | Entwickelt von Pädagogen!

D1920676

Klara Winter

Inhaltsübersicht

01 | THE LOST BALL – PRESENT SIMPLE 5

VOCABULARY 6
GAP TEXT 1: PRESENT SIMPLE COMPLETE THE SENTENCES WITH THE CORRECT FORM OF THE PRESENT SIMPLE: 7
ANSWER THE QUESTIONS ABOUT THE STORY 7
BRING THE WORDS INTO THE CORRECT ORDER 8
MATCH THE WORDS WITH THE CORRECT TRANSLATION 8
QUIZ 8
TRANSLATION: "DER VERLORENE BALL" 9

02 | THE BIG GAME – POSSESSIVE FORM WITH 'S, OF-GENITIVE, AND POSSESSIVE ADJECTIVES 13

VOCABULARY (ENGLISH - DEUTSCH) 14
GAP TEXT: POSSESSIVE FORM AND POSSESSIVE ADJECTIVES 15
ANSWER THE QUESTIONS ABOUT THE STORY 15
BRING THE WORDS INTO THE CORRECT ORDER 16
MATCH THE WORDS WITH THE CORRECT TRANSLATION 16
QUIZ 16
TRANSLATION: DAS GROSSE SPIEL 17

03 | THE LOST SHOES – ARTICLES (A, AN, THE) 21

VOCABULARY (ENGLISH - DEUTSCH) 22
GAP TEXT: ARTICLES (A, AN, THE) 22
ANSWER THE QUESTIONS ABOUT THE STORY 23
BRING THE WORDS INTO THE CORRECT ORDER 23
MATCH THE WORDS WITH THE CORRECT TRANSLATION 24
QUIZ 24
TRANSLATION: DIE VERLORENEN SCHUHE 25

04 | A BIG MISTAKE – HAVE AND HAS GOT 28

VOCABULARY (ENGLISH - DEUTSCH) 29
GAP TEXT: HAVE AND HAS GOT 30
ANSWER THE QUESTIONS ABOUT THE STORY 30
BRING THE WORDS INTO THE CORRECT ORDER 30
MATCH THE WORDS WITH THE CORRECT TRANSLATION 31
QUIZ 31
TRANSLATION: EIN GROSSER FEHLER 32

05 | AT THE STADIUM – DEMONSTRATIVE PRONOUNS: THIS, THAT, THESE, THOSE 35

VOCABULARY (ENGLISH - DEUTSCH) 36
GAP TEXT: DEMONSTRATIVE PRONOUNS (THIS/THAT/THESE/THOSE) 37
ANSWER THE QUESTIONS ABOUT THE STORY 37

Bring the words into the correct order 38
Match the words with the correct translation 38
Quiz 38
Translation: IM STADION 39

6 | THE TEAMWORK CHALLENGE – CAN AND MUST 42

Vocabulary (English - Deutsch) 43
Gap Text: Can and Must 44
Answer the questions about the story 44
Bring the words into the correct order 45
Match the words with the correct translation 45
Quiz 45
Translation: DIE TEAMWORK-HERAUSFORDERUNG 46

07 | IN WESTMINSTER ABBEY – DO AND DOES 50

Vocabulary (English - Deutsch) 52
Gap Text: Do and Does 52
Answer the questions about the story 53
Bring the words into the correct order 53
Match the words with the correct translation 53
Quiz 54
Translation: IN DER WESTMINSTER ABBEY 55

08 | TAKING THE BUS – QUESTION WORDS: WHERE, WHO, WHAT, HOW, WHY, WHEN 58

Vocabulary (English - Deutsch) 59
Gap Text: Question Words (Where, Who, What, How, Why, When) 60
Answer the questions about the story 60
Bring the words into the correct order 61
Match the words with the correct translation 61
Quiz 61
Translation: MIT DEM BUS 62

09 | AT THE TRAINING GROUND – PRESENT SIMPLE 66

Vocabulary (English - Deutsch) 67
Gap Text: Present Simple 68
Answer the questions about the story 69
Bring the words into the correct order 69
Match the words with the correct translation 69
Quiz 70
Translation: AUF DEM TRAININGSGELÄNDE 71

10 | THE FINAL MATCH – SIMPLE PAST 74

Vocabulary (English - Deutsch) 75
Gap Text: Simple Past 76

Answer the questions about the story 76
Bring the words into the correct order 77
Match the words with the correct translation 77
Quiz 77
Translation: DAS FINALE SPIEL 78

11 | THE LAST CLUE – SIMPLE PAST 82

Vocabulary (English - Deutsch) 84
Gap Text: Simple Past 84
Answer the questions about the story 85
Bring the words into the correct order 85
Match the words with the correct translation 85
Quiz 86
Translation: DER LETZTE HINWEIS 87

12 | THE SURPRISE GUEST – PRESENT CONTINUOUS 91

Vocabulary (English - Deutsch) 92
Gap Text: Present Continuous Complete the sentences with the correct form of the Present Continuous: 93
Answer the questions about the story 93
Bring the words into the correct order 94
Match the words with the correct translation 94
Quiz 94
Translation: Der Überraschungsgast 95

13 | THE UNEXPECTED RAIN – FUTURE SIMPLE 99

Vocabulary (English - Deutsch) 100
Gap Text: Future Simple 101
Answer the questions about the story 101
Bring the words into the correct order 101
Match the words with the correct translation 102
Quiz 102
Translation: Der unerwartete Regen 103

01 | THE LOST BALL – Present Simple

Lukas and Markus are 11 years old and live in Milan. Every afternoon, they go to the local park to play football with their friends. One day, after an intense match, they notice that their football is missing. Lukas looks around the field, but the ball is nowhere to be found.

"Where did it go?" Markus asks, confused.

They search the park, but the ball has disappeared. After some time, they spot a group of squirrels near the bushes, playing with something. Lukas and Markus run over and realize that the squirrels have taken their ball!

"They've stolen our football!" Lukas exclaims, half laughing.

Markus tries to grab the ball, but the squirrels are too quick. The boys laugh as they chase the squirrels around the park, trying to get their ball back. After a while, the squirrels drop the ball, and Lukas finally manages to pick it up.

"Got it!" he shouts, holding the ball high.

The boys return to the field, exhausted but happy to have their ball back. They continue playing, and this time, they make sure to keep a close eye on the ball.

Vocabulary

English	**Deutsch**
football	der Fußball
park	der Park
friends	die Freunde
squirrels	die Eichhörnchen
bushes	die Büsche
missing	verschwunden
to steal	stehlen
to chase	jagen
to laugh	lachen
to find	finden

Gap Text 1: Present Simple
Complete the sentences with the correct form of the Present Simple:

1. Lukas and Markus ____ (to be) 11 years old.
2. They ____ (to live) in Milan.
3. Every afternoon, they ____ (to play) football in the park.
4. One day, they ____ (to notice) their football is missing.
5. The squirrels ____ (to steal) their ball.
6. Lukas and Markus ____ (to chase) the squirrels.
7. The boys ____ (to laugh) as they run.
8. Finally, Lukas ____ (to grab) the ball.
9. They ____ (to return) to the field.
10. The boys ____ (to continue) playing football.

Answer the questions about the story

1. Where do Lukas and Markus live?
2. What do they do every afternoon?
3. What do they lose during the match?
4. Who steals their football?
5. Where do the boys find the ball?
6. What do they do after finding the ball?
7. How do they feel when they get the ball back?
8. Do the boys stop playing after the incident?
9. What do Lukas and Markus do to get their football back?

10. Why are Lukas and Markus happy at the end of the story?

Bring the words into the correct order

1. the / football / boys / play / the / in / park.
2. squirrels / ball / the / take / the.
3. Lukas / and / Markus / the / squirrels / chase.
4. laugh / they / as / run / the / boys.
5. finds / the / finally / Lukas / ball / the.

Match the words with the correct translation

Wörter (Englisch)	Übersetzungen (Deutsch)
1. Football	E. der Fußball
2. Park	C. der Park
3. Squirrels	B. die Eichhörnchen
4. Bushes	A. die Büsche
5. Steal	D. stehlen

Quiz

1. What do Lukas and Markus play in the park?
   - A) Basketball
   - B) Football
   - C) Tennis

2. Who takes their football?
    - A) Birds
    - B) Dogs
    - C) Squirrels
3. How do Lukas and Markus feel when they get their ball back?
    - A) Angry
    - B) Happy
    - C) Bored
4. Where do the boys chase the squirrels?
    - A) Around the park
    - B) In the city
    - C) On the street
5. What do the boys do after they find the ball?
    - A) Go home
    - B) Continue playing
    - C) Stop playing

Translation: "Der verlorene Ball"

Lukas und Markus sind 11 Jahre alt und leben in Mailand. Jeden Nachmittag gehen sie in den örtlichen Park, um mit ihren Freunden Fußball zu spielen. Eines Tages, nach einem intensiven Spiel, bemerken sie, dass ihr Fußball verschwunden ist. Lukas schaut sich auf dem Spielfeld um, aber der Ball ist nirgends zu finden.

"Wo ist er hin?" fragt Markus verwirrt.

Sie durchsuchen den Park, aber der Ball ist verschwunden. Nach einer Weile sehen sie eine Gruppe Eichhörnchen in der Nähe der Büsche, die mit etwas spielen. Lukas und Markus laufen hinüber und stellen fest, dass die Eichhörnchen ihren Ball genommen haben!

"Sie haben unseren Fußball gestohlen!" ruft Lukas, halb lachend.

Markus versucht, den Ball zu fangen, aber die Eichhörnchen sind zu schnell. Die Jungen lachen, während sie den Eichhörnchen im Park hinterherjagen und versuchen, ihren Ball zurückzubekommen. Schließlich lassen die Eichhörnchen den Ball fallen, und Lukas schafft es, ihn aufzuheben.

"Ich hab ihn!" ruft er und hält den Ball hoch.

Die Jungen kehren erschöpft, aber glücklich auf das Spielfeld zurück. Sie spielen weiter, und diesmal passen sie gut auf den Ball auf.

➢ Answers

Gap Text 1: Present Simple

1. are
2. live
3. play
4. notice
5. steal
6. chase

7. laugh
8. grabs
9. return
10. continue

Answer the questions about the story

1. Milan
2. Play football
3. Their football
4. Squirrels
5. Near the bushes
6. Continue playing football
7. Happy
8. No, they continue playing
9. They chase the squirrels
10. Because they have their football back

Bring the words into the correct order

1. The boys play football in the park.
2. The squirrels take the ball.
3. Lukas and Markus chase the squirrels.
4. The boys laugh as they run.
5. Finally, Lukas finds the ball.

Match the words with the correct translation

1. E | 2. C | 3. B | 4. A | 5. D

Quiz

1. B) Football
2. C) Squirrels
3. B) Happy
4. A) Around the park
5. B) Continue playing

02 | THE BIG GAME – Possessive Form with 'S, of-Genitive, and Possessive Adjectives

Lukas and Markus are excited. Today is the day of **the big game**. Their team, the Panthers, is playing against their biggest rivals, the Tigers. Lukas and Markus arrive at the field with their friends, ready to give it their all.

Lukas looks around and says, “Look, that’s **the Tigers’ coach**. He is talking to **his team**.”

Markus nods. “We’ve been practicing hard. **Our team** is ready for this match,” he says confidently.

The game starts, and it’s intense right from the beginning. The Tigers are fast and aggressive, but **the Panthers’ defense** is strong. Markus runs towards the goal and passes the ball to Lukas. With a powerful kick, Lukas scores the first goal of the match! The crowd cheers for **Lukas's goal**.

But the Tigers don't give up. In the second half, they score twice, making the score 2-1. With just a few minutes left, Lukas sees Markus near the goal. He passes the ball to **his friend**, and Markus kicks it hard. It's a goal! The Panthers tie the game at 2-2.

Now there's only one minute left. The Panthers have the ball. Lukas dribbles past two defenders and shoots. The ball flies past **the Tigers' goalkeeper**. It's a goal! The Panthers win 3-2.

After the game, the boys celebrate. "We did it!" Lukas says, high-fiving Markus. Their coach tells them, "I'm proud of **my team**. You played like champions today."

Vocabulary (English - Deutsch)

English	Deutsch
big game	das große Spiel
team	die Mannschaft
rival	der Rivale
coach	der Trainer
goal	das Tor
player	der Spieler
defense	die Abwehr

English	Deutsch
goalkeeper	der Torwart
to score	ein Tor schießen
to celebrate	feiern
to pass	passen
to shoot	schießen

Gap Text: Possessive Form and Possessive Adjectives

Complete the sentences with the correct form of possessives:

1. This is **Lukas's** team.
2. The Panthers play against **the Tigers'** team.
3. Lukas passes the ball to **his** friend Markus.
4. **The Tigers' goalkeeper** is quick, but Markus scores a goal.
5. The coach is proud of **his** team.

Answer the questions about the story

1. What is the name of Lukas and Markus's team?
2. Who scores the first goal of the match?
3. How many goals does the Tigers' team score?
4. What does Lukas do in the last minute of the game?
5. How do Lukas and Markus feel after the game?

Bring the words into the correct order

1. scores / goal / the / first / Lukas.
2. passes / ball / the / Lukas / Markus / to.
3. wins / team / game / the / Lukas's.
4. cheers / crowd / goal / for / Lukas's.
5. proud / coach / team / his / of / is.

Match the words with the correct translation

Words (English)	Translations (Deutsch)
1. Goal	E. das Tor
2. Team	B. die Mannschaft
3. Rival	D. der Rivale
4. Coach	C. der Trainer
5. Celebrate	A. feiern

Quiz

1. Who scores the first goal of the match?
    - A) Markus
    - B) Lukas
    - C) A player from the Tigers
2. What is the name of Lukas and Markus's team?
    - A) The Lions

- B) The Panthers
- C) The Tigers

3. How many goals do the Tigers score in the game?
   - A) One
   - B) Two
   - C) Three
4. What does Lukas do in the final minute of the game?
   - A) He scores the winning goal
   - B) He misses the shot
   - C) He passes the ball to Markus
5. How does the coach feel after the game?
   - A) Disappointed
   - B) Proud
   - C) Angry

Translation: DAS GROSSE SPIEL

Lukas und Markus sind aufgeregt. Heute ist der Tag des großen Spiels. Ihre Mannschaft, die Panthers, spielt gegen ihren größten Rivalen, die Tigers. Lukas und Markus kommen mit ihren Freunden am Spielfeld an und sind bereit, ihr Bestes zu geben.

Lukas schaut sich um und sagt: „Schau mal, das ist der Trainer der Tigers. Er spricht mit seiner Mannschaft."

Markus nickt. „Wir haben hart trainiert. Unsere Mannschaft ist bereit für dieses Spiel“, sagt er zuversichtlich.

Das Spiel beginnt und ist von Anfang an intensiv. Die Tigers sind schnell und aggressiv, aber die Verteidigung der Panthers ist stark. Markus läuft auf das Tor zu und passt den Ball zu Lukas. Mit einem kraftvollen Schuss erzielt Lukas das erste Tor des Spiels! Die Menge jubelt für Lukas's Tor.

Aber die Tigers geben nicht auf. In der zweiten Halbzeit erzielen sie zwei Tore, und das Ergebnis steht jetzt 2-1 für die Tigers. Nur noch wenige Minuten sind übrig, als Lukas Markus in der Nähe des Tors sieht. Er passt den Ball zu seinem Freund, und Markus schießt. Es ist ein Tor! Die Panthers gleichen zum 2-2 aus.

Jetzt bleibt nur noch eine Minute. Die Panthers haben den Ball. Lukas dribbelt an zwei Verteidigern vorbei und schießt. Der Ball fliegt an dem Torwart der Tigers vorbei. Es ist ein Tor! Die Panthers gewinnen 3-2.

Nach dem Spiel feiern die Jungs. „Wir haben es geschafft!“ sagt Lukas und gibt Markus einen High-Five. Ihr Trainer sagt ihnen: „Ich bin stolz auf meine Mannschaft. Ihr habt heute wie Champions gespielt.“

➢ Answers

Gap Text: Possessive Form and Possessive Adjectives

1. **is**
2. **play**
3. **passes**
4. **is, scores**
5. **is**

Answer the questions about the story

1. The Panthers
2. Lukas
3. Two
4. He scores the winning goal.
5. They feel happy and excited.

Bring the words into the correct order

1. Lukas scores the first goal.
2. Lukas passes the ball to Markus.
3. Lukas's team wins the game.
4. The crowd cheers for Lukas's goal.
5. The coach is proud of his team.

Match the words with the correct translation

1. E | 2. B | 3. D | 4. C | 5. A

Quiz

1. B) Lukas
2. B) The Panthers

3. B) Two
4. A) He scores the winning goal
5. B) Proud

03 | THE LOST SHOES – Articles (a, an, the)

Lukas and Markus are at the field, getting ready for another big match. But as they prepare to put on **their shoes**, Lukas notices something strange. "Where are my shoes?" he asks, looking around confused.

Markus looks at him and says, "Maybe you left **them** at home?"

Lukas shakes his head. "I'm sure I brought **them**. I had **them** in **my bag** before we left."

They search **the field**, looking under **the benches** and around **the goalposts**, but **Lukas's shoes** are nowhere to be found. Without **his shoes**, Lukas can't play.

Just as he's about to give up, one of **the younger players** runs over with **a big smile** on his face. "Are these your shoes?" he asks, holding up **a pair of blue shoes**.

"Yes! Thank you!" Lukas says, relieved. **The young boy** had found **the shoes** near **the locker room**.

With **his shoes** back on, Lukas and Markus are ready to start **the game**. They join **their teammates** on **the field**, and soon, **the match** begins. Lukas plays with renewed energy, grateful to have found **his shoes** just in time.

Vocabulary (English - Deutsch)

English	Deutsch
shoes	die Schuhe
bag	die Tasche
field	das Spielfeld
bench	die Bank
locker room	die Umkleidekabine
teammate	der Mitspieler
to search	suchen
to find	finden
to start	anfangen
to prepare	sich vorbereiten

Gap Text: Articles (a, an, the)

Complete the sentences with **a**, **an**, or **the**:

1. Lukas ____ (to look) for his shoes.
2. Markus ____ (to think) Lukas left them at ____ house.
3. They ____ (to search) around ____ field and under ____ bench.
4. ____ young player ____ (to find) Lukas's shoes.
5. With ____ shoes back, Lukas ____ (to be) ready for ____ game.

Answer the questions about the story

1. What does Lukas lose at the beginning of the story?
2. Where do Lukas and Markus search for the lost shoes?
3. Who finds Lukas's shoes?
4. Where were Lukas's shoes found?
5. How does Lukas feel after finding his shoes?

Bring the words into the correct order

1. lost / shoes / Lukas / his / has.
2. young / player / finds / Lukas’s / shoes / a.
3. field / the / around / they / search.
4. ready / is / the / Lukas / game / for.
5. thanks / boy / Lukas / the / young.

Match the words with the correct translation

Words (English)	Translations (Deutsch)
1. Shoes	E. die Schuhe
2. Bag	C. die Tasche
3. Field	A. das Spielfeld
4. Teammate	D. der Mitspieler
5. Locker room	B. die Umkleidekabine

Quiz

1. What does Lukas lose before the game?
    - A) His bag
    - B) His shoes
    - C) His jersey
2. Who finds Lukas's shoes?
    - A) Markus
    - B) A coach
    - C) A younger player
3. Where were the shoes found?
    - A) In the locker room
    - B) Near the bench
    - C) Near the goalpost
4. How does Lukas feel when he finds his shoes?
    - A) Angry

- B) Happy
- C) Bored

5. What do Lukas and Markus do after finding the shoes?
   - A) Go home
   - B) Start the game
   - C) Go to the locker room

Translation: DIE VERLORENEN SCHUHE

Lukas und Markus sind auf dem Spielfeld und bereiten sich auf ein weiteres großes Spiel vor. Aber als sie anfangen, ihre Schuhe anzuziehen, bemerkt Lukas etwas Seltsames. „Wo sind meine Schuhe?“ fragt er verwirrt, während er sich umschaut.

Markus sieht ihn an und sagt: „Vielleicht hast du sie zu Hause vergessen?“

Lukas schüttelt den Kopf. „Ich bin sicher, ich habe sie mitgebracht. Ich hatte sie in meiner Tasche, bevor wir losgegangen sind.“

Sie durchsuchen das Spielfeld, schauen unter den Bänken und um die Torpfosten herum, aber Lukass Schuhe sind nirgends zu finden. Ohne seine Schuhe kann Lukas nicht spielen.

Gerade als er aufgeben will, rennt einer der jüngeren Spieler mit einem großen Lächeln im Gesicht herüber. „Sind das deine Schuhe?“ fragt er und hält ein Paar blaue Schuhe hoch.

„Ja! Vielen Dank!“ sagt Lukas erleichtert. Der junge Junge hatte die Schuhe in der Nähe der Umkleidekabine gefunden.

Mit seinen Schuhen an den Füßen sind Lukas und Markus bereit, das Spiel zu beginnen. Sie schließen sich ihren Teamkollegen auf dem Spielfeld an, und bald beginnt das Spiel. Lukas spielt mit neuer Energie, dankbar, dass er seine Schuhe rechtzeitig gefunden hat.

➢ Answers

il Gap Text: Articles (a, an, the):

1. **Lukas is looking for his shoes.**
2. **Markus thinks Lukas left them at the house.**
3. **They search around the field and under the bench.**
4. **A young player finds Lukas's shoes.**
5. **With the shoes back, Lukas is ready for the game.**

Answer the questions about the story

1. His shoes
2. Around the field and under the bench
3. A younger player
4. Near the locker room
5. Relieved and happy

Bring the words into the correct order

1. Lukas has lost his shoes.
2. A young player finds Lukas's shoes.
3. They search around the field.
4. Lukas is ready for the game.

5. Lukas thanks the young boy.

Match the words with the correct translation

1. E | 2. C | 3. A | 4. D | 5. B

Quiz

1. B) His shoes
2. C) A younger player
3. B) Near the bench
4. B) Happy
5. B) Start the game

04 | A BIG MISTAKE – Have and Has Got

Lukas and Markus are at football practice. It's a hot day, and everyone is tired, but their coach has a special drill planned for them. "Today we'll work on passing and teamwork," the coach says. "Remember, a good team always helps each other."

The drill starts, and Lukas receives the ball. He looks around and sees Markus, wide open near the goal. "I've got to pass it to him!" Lukas thinks, but just as he kicks the ball, something goes wrong. Lukas accidentally passes the ball to one of the defenders from the other team!

The defender takes the ball and runs towards Lukas's goal. "I've made a big mistake!" Lukas says to himself, watching helplessly as the defender scores. Markus runs over to Lukas and pats him on the shoulder. "Don't worry, Lukas. Everyone makes mistakes. We've got time to win this game."

The coach calls the team over. "Lukas, you've got to keep your focus," he says kindly. "But don't be too hard on yourself. You've got the skills; you just need to use them at the right time."

Lukas nods, feeling a little better. The team starts again, and this time, Lukas passes the ball perfectly to Markus. Markus takes the shot, and it's a goal! The team cheers, and Lukas smiles. "I've got to trust myself more," he thinks.

Vocabulary (English - Deutsch)

English	Deutsch
mistake	der Fehler
defender	der Verteidiger
drill	die Übung
goal	das Tor
teamwork	die Teamarbeit
focus	die Konzentration
to pass	passen
to score	ein Tor schießen
to help	helfen
to trust	vertrauen

Gap Text: Have and Has Got

Complete the sentences with **have** or **has got**:

1. Lukas ____ (to have) good passing skills.
2. Markus ____ (to have) a strong shot.
3. The team ____ (to have) great teamwork.
4. Lukas ____ (to have) made a mistake during the game.
5. The coach says, "You ____ (to have) to stay focused."

Answer the questions about the story

1. What mistake does Lukas make during practice?
2. How does Markus help Lukas after his mistake?
3. What advice does the coach give Lukas?
4. What does Lukas do after making the mistake?
5. How does the team feel after Markus scores?

Bring the words into the correct order

1. makes / mistake / big / a / Lukas.
2. passes / the ball / Lukas / Markus / to.
3. got / focus / Lukas / has / to / his.
4. scores / Markus / a / goal.
5. got / trust / has / Lukas / himself / to.

Match the words with the correct translation

Words (English)	Translations (Deutsch)
1. Mistake	E. der Fehler
2. Teamwork	B. die Teamarbeit
3. Focus	D. die Konzentration
4. Drill	C. die Übung
5. Defender	A. der Verteidiger

Quiz

1. What mistake does Lukas make during the drill?
   - A) He passes the ball to the wrong player.
   - B) He misses a shot.
   - C) He forgets to run.
2. How does Markus help Lukas after his mistake?
   - A) He laughs at him.
   - B) He encourages him.
   - C) He ignores him.
3. What does the coach tell Lukas?
   - A) He needs to focus more.
   - B) He needs to run faster.
   - C) He needs to pass less.
4. What happens after Lukas makes a better pass?
   - A) Markus scores a goal.

- B) The other team scores.
- C) Lukas scores a goal.

5. How does Lukas feel after Markus scores?
    - A) Sad
    - B) Confident
    - C) Angry

Translation: EIN GROSSER FEHLER

Lukas und Markus sind beim Fußballtraining. Es ist ein heißer Tag, und alle sind müde, aber ihr Trainer hat eine besondere Übung für sie geplant. „Heute arbeiten wir am Passen und an der Teamarbeit“, sagt der Trainer. „Denkt daran, eine gute Mannschaft hilft sich immer gegenseitig.“

Die Übung beginnt, und Lukas bekommt den Ball. Er schaut sich um und sieht Markus, der ganz frei in der Nähe des Tores steht. „Ich muss zu ihm passen!“ denkt Lukas, aber als er den Ball tritt, geht etwas schief. Lukas passt den Ball versehentlich zu einem Verteidiger der anderen Mannschaft!

Der Verteidiger nimmt den Ball und rennt in Richtung Lukass Tor. „Ich habe einen großen Fehler gemacht!“ sagt Lukas zu sich selbst, während er hilflos zusieht, wie der Verteidiger ein Tor erzielt. Markus läuft zu Lukas und klopft ihm auf die Schulter. „Mach dir keine Sorgen, Lukas. Jeder macht Fehler. Wir haben noch Zeit, dieses Spiel zu gewinnen.“

Der Trainer ruft die Mannschaft zu sich. „Lukas, du musst konzentriert bleiben“, sagt er freundlich. „Aber sei nicht zu streng mit dir selbst. Du hast die Fähigkeiten, du musst sie nur zur richtigen Zeit einsetzen.“

Lukas nickt und fühlt sich ein wenig besser. Das Team startet erneut, und diesmal passt Lukas den Ball perfekt zu Markus. Markus schießt, und es ist ein Tor! Die Mannschaft jubelt, und Lukas lächelt. „Ich muss mir selbst mehr vertrauen“, denkt er.

➢ Answers

Gap Text:

1. has got
2. has got
3. has got
4. has
5. have

Answer the questions about the story

1. He passes the ball to the wrong player.
2. He encourages Lukas and tells him not to worry.
3. The coach tells Lukas to stay focused and not be too hard on himself.
4. Lukas makes a better pass to Markus, who scores.
5. The team is happy and excited after Markus scores.

Bring the words into the correct order

1. Lukas makes a big mistake.

2. Lukas passes the ball to Markus.
3. Lukas has got to focus.
4. Markus scores a goal.
5. Lukas has got to trust himself.

Match the words with the correct translation

1. E | 2. B | 3. D | 4. C | 5. A

Quiz

1. A) He passes the ball to the wrong player.
2. B) He encourages him.
3. A) He needs to focus more.
4. A) Markus scores a goal.
5. B) Confident

40

Hai detto:

sviluppa il capitolo 5

ChatGPT ha detto:

ChatGPT

05 | AT THE STADIUM – Demonstrative Pronouns: This, That, These, Those

It's a big day for Lukas and Markus. Their team has been invited to play a friendly match at a famous football stadium. When they arrive, they are amazed by how large and impressive it is. "Look at **this stadium**! It's huge!" Lukas says, pointing at the towering stands.

Markus nods. "Yeah, and look at **those seats** over there," he says, pointing to the top row. "I've never seen so many seats in my life!"

As they walk towards the field, their coach tells them, "We're going to play on **this field** today. Remember, it's just like any other field, so don't be nervous."

The boys look around, trying to take in everything. Markus notices a group of famous players warming up on the other side. "Hey, look at **those players**! They are the best in the league!" he says excitedly.

Lukas can't believe his eyes. "Do you think we could meet **those players** after the game?" he asks.

"I hope so!" Markus replies.

The match starts, and the boys quickly focus on their game. They feel a little nervous playing in such a big stadium, but soon, they get into their rhythm. Markus scores a goal, and the crowd cheers. "I'll never forget **this moment**," Markus says as they celebrate the goal.

Vocabulary (English - Deutsch)

English	Deutsch
stadium	das Stadion
seats	die Sitze
field	das Spielfeld
players	die Spieler
moment	der Moment
famous	berühmt
top row	die oberste Reihe
to play	spielen

English	Deutsch
to warm up	sich aufwärmen
to celebrate	feiern

Gap Text: Demonstrative Pronouns (This/That/These/Those)

Complete the sentences with **this**, **that**, **these**, or **those**:

1. Look at ____ stadium! It's huge.
2. Markus ____ (to point) to ____ seats at the top row.
3. The coach ____ (to say), "We're going to play on ____ field today."
4. "Can we meet ____ players after the game?" Lukas ____ (to ask).
5. "I'll never forget ____ moment," Markus ____ (to say) after scoring the goal.

Answer the questions about the story

1. Where is the team invited to play a match?
2. What impresses Lukas and Markus about the stadium?
3. What does Markus notice about the players warming up?
4. What does Lukas hope to do after the game?
5. How does Markus feel after scoring a goal?

Bring the words into the correct order

1. stadium / this / look / at / huge / is.
2. players / warming up / those / famous / are.
3. meet / players / those / we / can.
4. never / forget / this / I'll / moment.
5. score / Markus / goal / a / does.

Match the words with the correct translation

Words (English)	Translations (Deutsch)
1. Stadium	E. das Stadion
2. Seats	C. die Sitze
3. Players	B. die Spieler
4. Field	D. das Spielfeld
5. Famous	A. berühmt

Quiz

1. What do Lukas and Markus notice first when they enter the stadium?
   - A) The players
   - B) The seats
   - C) The size of the stadium
2. Who are the famous players warming up on the field?

- A) Players from the local team
- B) The best players in the league
- C) Coaches

3. What does the coach tell Lukas and Markus before the game?
   - A) To play hard
   - B) That it's just like any other field
   - C) To focus on the crowd
4. What happens during the match?
   - A) Markus scores a goal
   - B) Lukas scores a goal
   - C) The other team wins
5. How does Markus describe the moment after scoring the goal?
   - A) Amazing
   - B) Nervous
   - C) Unforgettable

Translation: IM STADION

Es ist ein großer Tag für Lukas und Markus. Ihre Mannschaft wurde eingeladen, ein Freundschaftsspiel in einem berühmten Fußballstadion zu spielen. Als sie ankommen, sind sie erstaunt, wie groß und beeindruckend es ist. „Schau dir **dieses Stadion** an! Es ist riesig!" sagt Lukas und zeigt auf die hohen Tribünen.

Markus nickt. „Ja, und schau dir **diese Sitze** dort oben an," sagt er und zeigt auf die oberste Reihe. „Ich habe noch nie in meinem Leben so viele Sitze gesehen!"

Als sie auf das Spielfeld gehen, sagt ihr Trainer: „Wir spielen heute auf **diesem Spielfeld**. Denkt daran, es ist wie jedes andere Spielfeld, also seid nicht nervös."

Die Jungs sehen sich um und versuchen, alles auf sich wirken zu lassen. Markus bemerkt eine Gruppe berühmter Spieler, die sich auf der anderen Seite aufwärmen. „Hey, schau dir **diese Spieler** an! Sie sind die Besten in der Liga!" sagt er aufgeregt.

Lukas kann seinen Augen kaum trauen. „Glaubst du, wir könnten **diese Spieler** nach dem Spiel treffen?" fragt er.

„Ich hoffe es!" antwortet Markus.

Das Spiel beginnt, und die Jungs konzentrieren sich schnell auf ihr eigenes Spiel. Sie sind ein bisschen nervös, in so einem großen Stadion zu spielen, aber bald finden sie ihren Rhythmus. Markus erzielt ein Tor, und die Menge jubelt. „Ich werde **diesen Moment** nie vergessen", sagt Markus, während sie das Tor feiern.

➢ Answers

Gap Text:

1. this
2. points, those
3. says, this

4. those, asks
5. this, says

Answer the questions about the story

1. At a famous football stadium
2. The size of the stadium and the many seats
3. That they are the best players in the league
4. Lukas hopes to meet the famous players after the game
5. Markus feels that the moment is unforgettable

Bring the words into the correct order

1. Look at this stadium, it is huge.
2. Those famous players are warming up.
3. Can we meet those players?
4. I'll never forget this moment.
5. Markus scores a goal.

Match the words with the correct translation

1. E | 2. C | 3. B | 4. D | 5. A

Quiz

1. C) The size of the stadium
2. B) The best players in the league
3. B) That it's just like any other field
4. A) Markus scores a goal
5. C) Unforgettable

6 | THE TEAMWORK CHALLENGE – Can and Must

It’s a rainy day, and Lukas and Markus’s team is about to face one of their toughest matches of the season. The field is wet, and the ball is slippery, but their coach has one clear message: "To win today, you **must** work together. No one can win this game alone. **You can** do it if you play as a team."

As the match begins, it becomes clear that the opposing team is very strong. They pass the ball quickly and have already scored a goal in the first few minutes. Lukas feels a little nervous. "We **must** score soon," he tells Markus.

Markus nods. "We **can** score, but we **must** keep our focus," he replies.

The coach shouts from the sideline, "Lukas, you **must** pass the ball! Don't try to do it all by yourself!"

Lukas listens to his coach and, the next time he gets the ball, he quickly passes it to Markus. Markus dribbles past two defenders and passes the ball back to Lukas. Together, they work their way up the field. Lukas is in front of the goal now. "You **can** score!" Markus shouts.

Lukas takes a deep breath and shoots. The ball flies past the goalkeeper and into the net. Goal!

The crowd cheers, and Lukas's teammates run over to celebrate. "That's what happens when we work together!" Markus says, high-fiving Lukas. "We **can** win this match if we keep playing like that."

By the end of the game, the team has worked together perfectly. They win 3-2, and their coach is proud. "Remember, you **can** achieve anything if you play as a team. Today, you showed what real teamwork looks like."

Vocabulary (English - Deutsch)

English	Deutsch
rainy	regnerisch
teamwork	die Teamarbeit
challenge	die Herausforderung
slippery	rutschig

English	Deutsch
defender	der Verteidiger
goal	das Tor
to win	gewinnen
to pass	passen
to shoot	schießen
to score	ein Tor schießen

Gap Text: Can and Must

Complete the sentences with **can** or **must**:

1. The coach says, "You ____ work together to win."
2. Lukas thinks, "We ____ score soon."
3. Markus says, "We ____ win if we stay focused."
4. The coach tells Lukas, "You ____ pass the ball."
5. Markus shouts, "You ____ score!"

Answer the questions about the story

1. What does the coach say is necessary to win the game?
2. How does the opposing team start the game?
3. What advice does Markus give Lukas during the game?
4. What happens after Lukas and Markus work together?
5. How does the team feel after winning the match?

Bring the words into the correct order

1. pass / must / the ball / Lukas.
2. can / win / we / the game.
3. score / must / we / soon.
4. teamwork / must / play / with / we.
5. can / Markus / says / we / win.

Match the words with the correct translation

Words (English)	Translations (Deutsch)
1. Rainy	E. regnerisch
2. Challenge	D. die Herausforderung
3. Slippery	A. rutschig
4. Defender	C. der Verteidiger
5. Teamwork	B. die Teamarbeit

Quiz

1. What does the coach tell the team before the game?
   - A) To score quickly
   - B) To work as a team
   - C) To pass the ball less
2. How does the opposing team play at the start of the game?

- A) Slowly
- B) Aggressively
- C) They score quickly

3. What does Lukas do after hearing the coach's advice?
    - A) He passes the ball to Markus
    - B) He tries to score by himself
    - C) He waits too long to pass
4. What does Markus tell Lukas during the game?
    - A) You can pass to someone else
    - B) You can score!
    - C) You must defend
5. How does the team win the game?
    - A) By working together
    - B) By playing aggressively
    - C) By making fewer mistakes

Translation: DIE TEAMWORK-HERAUSFORDERUNG

Es ist ein regnerischer Tag, und Lukas und Markuss Mannschaft steht vor einem der härtesten Spiele der Saison. Der Platz ist nass, und der Ball ist rutschig, aber ihr Trainer hat eine klare Botschaft: "Um heute zu gewinnen, **müsst** ihr zusammenarbeiten. Niemand kann dieses Spiel allein gewinnen. **Ihr könnt** es schaffen, wenn ihr als Team spielt."

Als das Spiel beginnt, wird schnell klar, dass die gegnerische Mannschaft sehr stark ist. Sie passen den Ball schnell und haben schon in den ersten Minuten ein Tor erzielt. Lukas ist ein wenig nervös. "Wir **müssen** bald ein Tor schießen", sagt er zu Markus.

Markus nickt. "Wir **können** ein Tor schießen, aber wir **müssen** konzentriert bleiben", antwortet er.

Der Trainer ruft von der Seitenlinie: "Lukas, du **musst** den Ball abgeben! Versuch nicht, alles allein zu machen!"

Lukas hört auf seinen Trainer und passt den Ball beim nächsten Mal schnell zu Markus. Markus dribbelt an zwei Verteidigern vorbei und passt den Ball zurück zu Lukas. Gemeinsam arbeiten sie sich nach vorne. Lukas steht jetzt vor dem Tor. "Du **kannst** ein Tor schießen!" ruft Markus.

Lukas holt tief Luft und schießt. Der Ball fliegt am Torwart vorbei und ins Netz. Tor!

Die Menge jubelt, und Lukass Teamkollegen rennen herbei, um zu feiern. "Das passiert, wenn wir zusammenarbeiten!" sagt Markus und gibt Lukas ein High-Five. "Wir **können** dieses Spiel gewinnen, wenn wir so weiterspielen."

Am Ende des Spiels hat das Team perfekt zusammengearbeitet. Sie gewinnen 3-2, und ihr Trainer ist stolz. "Denkt daran, ihr **könnt** alles erreichen, wenn ihr als Team spielt. Heute habt ihr gezeigt, was echte Teamarbeit bedeutet."

➢ Answers

Gap Text:

1. must
2. must
3. can
4. must
5. can

Answer the questions about the story

1. They must work together.
2. They score quickly.
3. They must stay focused.
4. They score a goal together.
5. They feel proud and excited.

Bring the words into the correct order

1. Lukas must pass the ball.
2. We can win the game.
3. We must score soon.
4. We must play with teamwork.
5. Markus says we can win.

Match the words with the correct translation

1. E | 2. D | 3. A | 4. C | 5. B

Quiz

1. B) To work as a team
2. C) They score quickly

3. A) He passes the ball to Markus
4. B) You can score!
5. A) By working together

07 | IN WESTMINSTER ABBEY – Do and Does

Lukas and Markus are on a special trip to London with their football team. After a successful season, their coach has arranged for them to visit one of the most famous landmarks in the city: Westminster Abbey. The boys are excited, not just because they get to explore London, but also because there is a special surprise waiting for them.

As they enter Westminster Abbey, their coach gathers them together. "Today, we are not only going to learn about history," he says, "but we also have a mystery to solve. You **do** need to pay attention to every detail inside this beautiful place, because hidden inside is a clue that could lead us to a special reward."

Lukas raises his hand. "What **does** the clue look like?" he asks, curious.

Their coach smiles. "You'll have to find out for yourselves. Work together, ask questions, and observe everything."

The boys start walking through the Abbey, looking at the statues, paintings, and ancient tombs. "Wow, this place **does** have a lot of history," Markus says as they stop to admire the tomb of a famous king.

"Yes, it **does**," Lukas replies, thinking hard. "Do you think the clue is near one of these statues?"

"Maybe, but what **does** the coach mean by a special reward?" Markus wonders aloud.

As they continue their search, Lukas notices something unusual near a statue of a knight. "Hey, Markus, **do** you see that symbol on the knight's shield?" he asks. "It looks different from the others."

Markus nods. "Yes, it **does**! Let's ask the coach if this could be the clue."

They rush over to their coach, who smiles when he sees what they found. "You've solved the mystery," he says proudly. "Now, because you worked together and used your curiosity, we're heading to the surprise: a special visit to a professional football team's training ground tomorrow!"

The boys cheer. "This trip **does** get better and better!" Lukas says happily.

Vocabulary (English - Deutsch)

English	Deutsch
statue	die Statue
tomb	das Grab
shield	der Schild
mystery	das Rätsel
clue	der Hinweis
reward	die Belohnung
knight	der Ritter
to admire	bewundern
to solve	lösen
to ask	fragen

Gap Text: Do and Does

Complete the sentences with **do** or **does**:

1. ____ the coach ____ (to have) a special surprise for the team?
2. Lukas and Markus ____ (to want) to find the clue.
3. "What ____ the clue ____ (to look) like?" Lukas asks.
4. The boys ____ (to admire) the history in Westminster Abbey.

5. "___ you ___ (to see) that symbol on the knight's shield?" Lukas asks Markus.

Answer the questions about the story

1. Where does Lukas and Markus's team go on their special trip?
2. What challenge does the coach give the team at Westminster Abbey?
3. What question does Lukas ask the coach?
4. What do Lukas and Markus find near the statue of a knight?
5. What is the special reward for solving the mystery?

Bring the words into the correct order

1. coach / does / have / a / special / what / surprise?
2. find / boys / the / clue / do.
3. does / the / look / clue / what / like?
4. do / they / the / statue / admire.
5. does / that / see / do / symbol / you?

Match the words with the correct translation

Words (English) Translations (Deutsch)

1. Statue D. die Statue

Words (English) Translations (Deutsch)

2. Clue	A. der Hinweis
3. Reward	E. die Belohnung
4. Shield	B. der Schild
5. Mystery	C. das Rätsel

Quiz

1. Where do Lukas and Markus visit with their team?
    - A) Buckingham Palace
    - B) Westminster Abbey
    - C) The Tower of London
2. What does the coach tell the boys to do inside Westminster Abbey?
    - A) Take pictures
    - B) Look for a hidden clue
    - C) Find a statue of a famous king
3. What do Lukas and Markus discover near the statue of a knight?
    - A) A hidden message
    - B) A special shield with a symbol
    - C) A locked chest
4. What is the reward for solving the mystery?
    - A) A visit to a football team's training ground

- B) A new football
- C) A historical tour

5. How do the boys feel after solving the mystery?
   - A) Confused
   - B) Excited
   - C) Disappointed

Translation: IN DER WESTMINSTER ABBEY

Lukas und Markus sind mit ihrer Fußballmannschaft auf einer besonderen Reise nach London. Nach einer erfolgreichen Saison hat ihr Trainer für sie eine Besichtigung eines der berühmtesten Wahrzeichen der Stadt arrangiert: der Westminster Abbey. Die Jungs sind aufgeregt, nicht nur, weil sie London erkunden können, sondern auch, weil sie wissen, dass eine besondere Überraschung auf sie wartet.

Als sie die Westminster Abbey betreten, versammelt der Trainer sie um sich. "Heute werden wir nicht nur etwas über Geschichte lernen", sagt er, "sondern wir haben auch ein Rätsel zu lösen. Ihr **müsst** auf jedes Detail achten, denn irgendwo hier drin ist ein Hinweis versteckt, der uns zu einer besonderen Belohnung führen könnte."

Lukas hebt die Hand. "Wie **sieht** der Hinweis aus?" fragt er neugierig.

Ihr Trainer lächelt. "Das müsst ihr selbst herausfinden. Arbeitet zusammen, stellt Fragen und beobachtet alles."

Die Jungs beginnen, durch die Abbey zu gehen, und schauen sich die Statuen, Gemälde und alten Gräber an. „Wow, dieser Ort **hat** eine Menge Geschichte“, sagt Markus, als sie vor dem Grab eines berühmten Königs stehen bleiben.

„Ja, das **hat** er“, antwortet Lukas und denkt angestrengt nach. „Denkst du, der Hinweis ist in der Nähe einer dieser Statuen?“

„Vielleicht, aber was **meint** der Trainer mit einer besonderen Belohnung?“ fragt sich Markus laut.

Als sie weiter suchen, bemerkt Lukas etwas Ungewöhnliches an einer Statue eines Ritters. „Hey, Markus, **siehst** du dieses Symbol auf dem Schild des Ritters?“ fragt er. „Es sieht anders aus als die anderen.“

Markus nickt. „Ja, das **tut** es! Lass uns den Trainer fragen, ob das der Hinweis sein könnte.“

Sie rennen zu ihrem Trainer, der lächelt, als er sieht, was sie gefunden haben. "Ihr habt das Rätsel gelöst", sagt er stolz. "Weil ihr zusammengearbeitet und eure Neugier genutzt habt, erwartet euch morgen eine besondere Überraschung: ein Besuch auf dem Trainingsgelände einer Profifußballmannschaft!"

Die Jungs jubeln. „Diese Reise **wird** immer besser!“ sagt Lukas glücklich.

➢ Answers

Gap Text:

1. **Does, have**

2. **do**
3. **does, look**
4. **do**
5. **Do, see**

Answer the questions about the story

1. Westminster Abbey
2. To find a hidden clue
3. "What does the clue look like?"
4. A special symbol on a knight's shield
5. A visit to a professional football team's training ground

Bring the words into the correct order

1. What does the coach have as a special surprise?
2. The boys do find the clue.
3. What does the clue look like?
4. They do admire the statue.
5. Do you see that symbol?

Match the words with the correct translation

1. D | 2. A | 3. E | 4. B | 5. C

Quiz

1. B) Westminster Abbey
2. B) Look for a hidden clue
3. B) A special shield with a symbol
4. A) A visit to a football team's training ground
5. B) Excited

08 | TAKING THE BUS – Question Words: Where, Who, What, How, Why, When

After their exciting day at Westminster Abbey, Lukas, Markus, and their team are ready for another adventure in London. Today, they're going to visit a professional football team's training ground. But first, they need to take a bus across the city.

The boys gather at the bus stop, excited but a little confused. "Where **is the bus stop**?" Lukas asks, looking around.

"It's right here," Markus says, pointing at the sign. "But **when** does the bus come?"

The coach checks his watch and smiles. "The bus arrives in 10 minutes, so we have some time."

As they wait, Markus notices something unusual. "Who **are those people** over there?" he asks, pointing to a group of fans dressed in football jerseys.

"They're probably here to see their favorite team," Lukas replies. "But **what** are they waiting for?"

Just then, a large double-decker bus pulls up, and the doors open. "This is our bus," the coach says. "Now, let's get on board!"

The boys climb onto the bus and head for the upper deck. They sit by the window, excited to see the sights of London as they travel to the training ground. Markus looks out and says, "Wow, look at **how** tall that building is! London is amazing."

Lukas nods, still curious about the football fans. "Why **do they love football** so much?" he wonders.

"I don't know," Markus says, "but I guess it's the same reason we do."

After a fun bus ride, they finally arrive at the training ground. "We made it!" Lukas says, jumping off the bus. "Now, let's go see **who** we get to meet today."

Vocabulary (English - Deutsch)

English	Deutsch
bus stop	die Bushaltestelle
football team	die Fußballmannschaft
fan	der Fan

English	Deutsch
building	das Gebäude
double-decker bus	der Doppeldeckerbus
upper deck	das Oberdeck
to wait	warten
to arrive	ankommen
to travel	reisen
to wonder	sich fragen

Gap Text: Question Words (Where, Who, What, How, Why, When)

Complete the sentences with the correct **question words**:

1. ____ does the bus arrive?
2. ____ are those people over there?
3. ____ is the bus stop?
4. ____ are they waiting for?
5. ____ do they love football so much?
6. ____ tall is that building?

Answer the questions about the story

1. Where are Lukas, Markus, and their team going today?
2. What does Lukas ask when they arrive at the bus stop?

3. Who does Markus notice while waiting for the bus?
4. How long do they have to wait for the bus to arrive?
5. Why does Lukas wonder about the football fans?

Bring the words into the correct order

1. bus / the / when / does / arrive?
2. fans / those / who / are / over there?
3. what / are / they / for / waiting?
4. tall / how / building / that / is?
5. bus / the / where / stop / is?

Match the words with the correct translation

Words (English)	Translations (Deutsch)
1. Bus stop	E. die Bushaltestelle
2. Fan	D. der Fan
3. Double-decker bus	A. der Doppeldeckerbus
4. Building	B. das Gebäude
5. Travel	C. reisen

Quiz

1. Where does the bus take the team?
   - A) To the hotel

- B) To a professional football team's training ground
- C) To the stadium

2. What does Markus notice while they wait for the bus?
    - A) A group of football fans
    - B) A strange building
    - C) A famous player
3. How long do they wait for the bus to arrive?
    - A) 5 minutes
    - B) 10 minutes
    - C) 15 minutes
4. Where do the boys sit on the bus?
    - A) On the upper deck
    - B) Near the driver
    - C) In the back row
5. What does Lukas wonder about the football fans?
    - A) Why they love football so much
    - B) Where they are going
    - C) What team they support

Translation: MIT DEM BUS

Nach ihrem aufregenden Tag in der Westminster Abbey sind Lukas, Markus und ihr Team bereit für ein weiteres Abenteuer in London. Heute besuchen sie das Trainingsgelände einer

Profifußballmannschaft. Aber zuerst müssen sie mit dem Bus quer durch die Stadt fahren.

Die Jungs versammeln sich an der Bushaltestelle, aufgeregt, aber ein bisschen verwirrt. „Wo **ist die Bushaltestelle**?“ fragt Lukas und schaut sich um.

„Sie ist genau hier“, sagt Markus und zeigt auf das Schild. „Aber **wann** kommt der Bus?“

Der Trainer schaut auf seine Uhr und lächelt. „Der Bus kommt in 10 Minuten, also haben wir noch etwas Zeit.“

Während sie warten, bemerkt Markus etwas Ungewöhnliches. „Wer **sind diese Leute** dort drüben?“ fragt er und zeigt auf eine Gruppe Fans, die Fußballtrikots tragen.

„Sie sind wahrscheinlich hier, um ihre Lieblingsmannschaft zu sehen“, antwortet Lukas. „Aber **was** warten sie?“

In diesem Moment hält ein großer Doppeldeckerbus an, und die Türen öffnen sich. „Das ist unser Bus“, sagt der Trainer. „Lasst uns einsteigen!“

Die Jungs steigen in den Bus und gehen zum Oberdeck. Sie setzen sich ans Fenster und freuen sich darauf, die Sehenswürdigkeiten Londons zu sehen, während sie zum Trainingsgelände fahren. Markus schaut hinaus und sagt: „Wow, schau mal, **wie** hoch dieses Gebäude ist! London ist unglaublich.“

Lukas nickt, immer noch neugierig über die Fußballfans. „Warum **lieben sie Fußball** so sehr?“ fragt er sich.

„Ich weiß es nicht“, sagt Markus, „aber ich schätze, es ist der gleiche Grund, warum wir es tun.“

Nach einer lustigen Busfahrt kommen sie endlich am Trainingsgelände an. „Wir haben es geschafft!“ sagt Lukas, als er aus dem Bus springt. „Jetzt lasst uns sehen, **wen** wir heute treffen dürfen.“

➢ Answers

Gap Text:

1. When
2. Who
3. Where
4. What
5. Why
6. How

Answer the questions about the story

1. To visit a professional football team’s training ground
2. He asks where the bus stop is
3. He notices a group of football fans
4. They wait 10 minutes for the bus
5. Because he wonders why they love football so much

Bring the words into the correct order

1. When does the bus arrive?
2. Who are those fans over there?
3. What are they waiting for?
4. How tall is that building?

5. Where is the bus stop?

Match the words with the correct translation

1. E | 2. D | 3. A | 4. B | 5. C

Quiz

1. B) To a professional football team's training ground
2. A) A group of football fans
3. B) 10 minutes
4. A) On the upper deck
5. A) Why they love football so much

09 | AT THE TRAINING GROUND – Present Simple

Lukas, Markus, and their teammates have finally arrived at the professional football team's training ground. It's a dream come true for the boys. They can't wait to see how professional players train and to learn from the best.

The coach gathers the team near the entrance. "Remember," he says, "today you're here to observe and learn. **They train** every day to become great players, and we **want** to learn from them."

As the boys walk onto the training ground, they see the players warming up. "Wow," Markus says, "look at how fast **they run**. **They do** everything so quickly!"

Lukas nods in agreement. "Yes, and **they pass** the ball so smoothly," he adds.

The boys sit on the side, watching the pros practice. One of the players kicks a ball toward them, and Lukas quickly stands up to pass it back. "Great pass," one of the players says with a smile.

"Thanks!" Lukas says, feeling proud.

Markus turns to the coach and asks, "Do you think we can ever train like that?"

The coach smiles. "Yes, but it takes hard work. **They practice** every day, and so **must** we."

After watching the practice, the boys get a chance to meet some of the players. "Do **you play** football at school?" one of the players asks Lukas.

"Yes, we **play** every day after school," Lukas replies excitedly. "We want to be as good as you one day."

"Keep practicing," the player says, "and you can achieve anything."

By the end of the day, the boys are inspired. "I can't wait to get back to training," Markus says. "Watching these players makes me want to work harder."

Lukas agrees. "Yes, I want to practice more and get better every day. **We play** as a team, and one day we might be just like them."

Vocabulary (English - Deutsch)

English	Deutsch

English	Deutsch
training ground	das Trainingsgelände
practice	das Training
to observe	beobachten
to learn	lernen
to pass	passen
to run	laufen
to play	spielen
hard work	harte Arbeit
smoothly	reibungslos
professional	professionell

Gap Text: Present Simple

Complete the sentences with the correct form of the **Present Simple**:

1. The professional players ____ (to train) every day.
2. Lukas and Markus ____ (to want) to become better footballers.
3. The boys ____ (to watch) the players warm up.
4. One of the players ____ (to kick) the ball towards Lukas.
5. Lukas and Markus ____ (to play) football at school.

Answer the questions about the story

1. Where do Lukas and Markus visit with their team?
2. What do the boys do when they arrive at the training ground?
3. How do the professional players practice?
4. What does Lukas do when the ball comes toward him?
5. How do Lukas and Markus feel after watching the players?

Bring the words into the correct order

1. players / every day / train / the.
2. watch / practice / boys / the / the.
3. smoothly / ball / they / pass / the.
4. we / football / every day / play.
5. want / Lukas / better / to get / and Markus.

Match the words with the correct translation

Words (English)	Translations (Deutsch)
1. Practice	C. das Training
2. Professional	E. professionell
3. Pass	B. passen
4. Hard work	D. harte Arbeit
5. Training ground	A. das Trainingsgelände

Quiz

1. Where do Lukas, Markus, and their team go?
    - A) To a stadium
    - B) To a professional football team's training ground
    - C) To a football camp
2. What do the boys notice about the professional players?
    - A) They train slowly
    - B) They train quickly and smoothly
    - C) They only play for fun
3. What happens when the ball comes toward Lukas?
    - A) He catches it
    - B) He passes it back
    - C) He misses it
4. What do Lukas and Markus do every day after school?
    - A) They play football
    - B) They go swimming
    - C) They watch football matches
5. How do the boys feel after watching the professional players?
    - A) Bored
    - B) Inspired
    - C) Tired

Translation: AUF DEM TRAININGSGELÄNDE

Lukas, Markus und ihre Teamkollegen sind endlich auf dem Trainingsgelände einer Profifußballmannschaft angekommen. Es ist ein wahr gewordener Traum für die Jungs. Sie können es kaum erwarten, zu sehen, wie Profis trainieren und von den Besten zu lernen.

Der Trainer versammelt die Mannschaft am Eingang. "Denkt daran", sagt er, "heute seid ihr hier, um zu beobachten und zu lernen. **Sie trainieren** jeden Tag, um großartige Spieler zu werden, und wir **wollen** von ihnen lernen."

Als die Jungs auf das Trainingsgelände gehen, sehen sie, wie sich die Spieler aufwärmen. "Wow," sagt Markus, "schau, wie schnell **sie laufen**. **Sie machen** alles so schnell!"

Lukas nickt zustimmend. "Ja, und **sie passen** den Ball so reibungslos," fügt er hinzu.

Die Jungs setzen sich an die Seite und sehen den Profis beim Training zu. Einer der Spieler schießt den Ball in ihre Richtung, und Lukas steht schnell auf, um ihn zurückzupassen. "Guter Pass," sagt einer der Spieler mit einem Lächeln.

"Danke!" sagt Lukas stolz.

Markus wendet sich an den Trainer und fragt: "Glaubst du, wir können jemals so trainieren?"

Der Trainer lächelt. "Ja, aber das erfordert harte Arbeit. **Sie trainieren** jeden Tag, und das **müssen** wir auch."

Nachdem sie das Training gesehen haben, bekommen die Jungs die Gelegenheit, einige der Spieler zu treffen. "Spielst **du** Fußball in der Schule?" fragt einer der Spieler Lukas.

"Ja, wir **spielen** jeden Tag nach der Schule," antwortet Lukas aufgeregt. "Wir wollen eines Tages so gut sein wie ihr."

"Bleibt dran und übt weiter," sagt der Spieler, "dann könnt ihr alles erreichen."

Am Ende des Tages sind die Jungs voller neuer Energie. "Ich kann es kaum erwarten, wieder zu trainieren," sagt Markus. "Diese Spieler zu sehen, motiviert mich, noch härter zu arbeiten."

Lukas stimmt zu. "Ja, ich will mehr trainieren und jeden Tag besser werden. **Wir spielen** als Team, und eines Tages sind wir vielleicht genauso gut wie sie."

➢ Answers

Gap Text:

1. train
2. want
3. watch
4. kicks
5. play

Answer the questions about the story

1. They visit a professional football team's training ground.
2. They watch the players warm up and observe the practice.
3. They train quickly and pass the ball smoothly.

4. Lukas stands up and passes it back.
5. They feel inspired and excited to improve.

Bring the words into the correct order

1. The players train every day.
2. The boys watch the practice.
3. They pass the ball smoothly.
4. We play football every day.
5. Lukas and Markus want to get better.

Match the words with the correct translation

1. C | 2. E | 3. B | 4. D | 5. A

Quiz

1. B) To a professional football team's training ground
2. B) They train quickly and smoothly
3. B) He passes it back
4. A) They play football
5. B) Inspired

10 | THE FINAL MATCH – Simple Past

It's the day of the final match. Lukas and Markus have worked hard all season, and now it's time to face their biggest challenge yet. They arrive at the stadium, nervous but excited. Their coach gathers them around and says, "You've trained for this moment. Today, you play your best game ever."

As the game begins, Lukas remembers everything they practiced. In the first few minutes, Markus **passed** him the ball, and Lukas **ran** down the field as fast as he could. He **looked** up and saw the goalkeeper coming toward him. With a powerful kick, Lukas **scored** the first goal of the match! The crowd **cheered** loudly, and Lukas's teammates **celebrated** around him.

But the other team **did not give up** easily. After Lukas's goal, the opponents quickly **recovered** and **scored** two goals before halftime. "We **need** to stay focused," the coach told them during the break. "You **played** well, but you can do even better in the second half."

When the second half started, the game became more intense. Markus **passed** the ball to Lukas again, and this time, Lukas **decided** to pass it to another teammate. They **worked** together, and soon they **scored** another goal, tying the match at 2-2.

With only a few minutes left, Lukas **stole** the ball from an opponent and **rushed** toward the goal. Everyone held their breath as Lukas **kicked** the ball with all his strength. It **flew** past the goalkeeper and into the net. Goal! The final whistle **blew**, and Lukas's team **won** the game 3-2. The stadium **erupted** in cheers as the team celebrated their victory.

After the game, the coach said, "I'm proud of all of you. You **worked** hard, you **never gave up**, and you **played** like champions."

Lukas and Markus hugged each other. "We **did** it!" Markus said, grinning. "All that hard work **paid off**."

"Yes," Lukas replied, smiling. "This is a day we'll never forget."

Vocabulary (English - Deutsch)

English	Deutsch
final match	das Endspiel

English	Deutsch
opponent	der Gegner
goal	das Tor
teammate	der Mitspieler
whistle	die Pfeife
victory	der Sieg
to pass	passen
to kick	schießen
to score	ein Tor schießen
to celebrate	feiern

Gap Text: Simple Past

Complete the sentences with the correct form of the **Simple Past**:

1. Lukas ____ (to score) the first goal of the match.
2. The crowd ____ (to cheer) when Lukas's team scored.
3. The other team ____ (to score) two goals before halftime.
4. Markus ____ (to pass) the ball to Lukas during the match.
5. Lukas's team ____ (to win) the final match.

Answer the questions about the story

1. What happened in the first few minutes of the match?
2. How did the other team respond after Lukas's goal?

3. What did the coach say to the team at halftime?
4. What happened in the final minutes of the match?
5. How did Lukas and Markus feel after winning the match?

Bring the words into the correct order

1. scored / Lukas / the / goal / first.
2. ball / passed / Markus / Lukas / to / the.
3. won / match / the / team / final / the.
4. team / celebrated / the / victory / their.
5. cheered / the / crowd / goal / the / after.

Match the words with the correct translation

Words (English)	Translations (Deutsch)
1. Final match	A. das Endspiel
2. Opponent	C. der Gegner
3. Whistle	D. die Pfeife
4. Victory	B. der Sieg
5. Teammate	E. der Mitspieler

Quiz

1. How did Lukas score the first goal of the match?
   - A) He passed the ball
   - B) He kicked the ball past the goalkeeper

- C) He missed the shot

2. What did the other team do after Lukas's goal?
   - A) They gave up
   - B) They scored two goals
   - C) They got tired
3. What did Lukas do in the final minutes of the match?
   - A) He passed the ball to Markus
   - B) He stole the ball and scored the winning goal
   - C) He missed the last shot
4. How did Lukas's team win the final match?
   - A) By scoring in the last minute
   - B) By scoring three goals in the first half
   - C) By winning in extra time
5. What did the coach say after the match?
   - A) "You could have played better."
   - B) "You played like champions."
   - C) "You need to practice more."

Translation: DAS FINALE SPIEL

Es ist der Tag des Endspiels. Lukas und Markus haben die ganze Saison hart gearbeitet, und jetzt stehen sie vor ihrer größten Herausforderung. Sie kommen nervös, aber aufgeregt im Stadion an. Ihr Trainer versammelt sie und sagt: "Ihr habt für diesen Moment trainiert. Heute spielt ihr euer bestes Spiel."

Als das Spiel beginnt, erinnert sich Lukas an alles, was sie geübt haben. In den ersten Minuten **passte** Markus ihm den Ball, und Lukas **rannte** so schnell er konnte über das Spielfeld. Er **schaute** hoch und sah den Torwart auf ihn zukommen. Mit einem kraftvollen Schuss **schoss** Lukas das erste Tor des Spiels! Die Menge **jubelte** laut, und Lukass Teamkollegen **feierten** mit ihm.

Aber die andere Mannschaft **gab nicht auf**. Nach Lukass Tor **erholte** sich der Gegner schnell und **schoss** zwei Tore vor der Halbzeit. "Wir **müssen** konzentriert bleiben", sagte der Trainer in der Pause. "Ihr **habt gut gespielt**, aber in der zweiten Hälfte könnt ihr noch besser sein."

Als die zweite Halbzeit begann, wurde das Spiel intensiver. Markus **passte** den Ball wieder zu Lukas, aber diesmal **entschied** sich Lukas, ihn zu einem anderen Teamkollegen zu passen. Sie **arbeiteten** zusammen, und bald **schossen** sie ein weiteres Tor, das Spiel stand jetzt 2-2.

Mit nur noch wenigen Minuten auf der Uhr **stibitzte** Lukas den Ball von einem Gegner und **eilte** auf das Tor zu. Alle hielten den Atem an, als Lukas den Ball mit aller Kraft **schoss**. Er **flog** am Torwart vorbei und ins Netz. Tor! Der Schlusspfiff **erschallte**, und Lukass Team **gewann** das Spiel 3-2. Das Stadion **brach in Jubel aus**, als das Team ihren Sieg feierte.

Nach dem Spiel sagte der Trainer: "Ich bin stolz auf euch. Ihr **habt hart gearbeitet**, ihr **habt niemals aufgegeben** und ihr **habt wie Champions gespielt**."

Lukas und Markus umarmten sich. "Wir **haben es geschafft**!" sagte Markus mit einem breiten Grinsen. "Die ganze harte Arbeit **hat sich ausgezahlt**."

"Ja," antwortete Lukas lächelnd. "Das ist ein Tag, den wir nie vergessen werden."

➢ Answers

Gap Text:

1. scored
2. cheered
3. scored
4. passed
5. won

Answer the questions about the story

1. Lukas scored the first goal after Markus passed him the ball.
2. They quickly recovered and scored two goals.
3. The coach said they played well but could do better in the second half.
4. Lukas stole the ball and scored the winning goal.
5. They felt proud and excited.

Bring the words into the correct order

1. Lukas scored the first goal.
2. Markus passed the ball to Lukas.

3. The team won the final match.
4. The team celebrated their victory.
5. The crowd cheered after the goal.

Match the words with the correct translation

1. A | 2. C | 3. D | 4. B | 5. E

Quiz

1. B) He kicked the ball past the goalkeeper
2. B) They scored two goals
3. B) He stole the ball and scored the winning goal
4. A) By scoring in the last minute
5. B) "You played like champions."

11 | THE LAST CLUE – Simple Past

After their incredible season and final match victory, Lukas, Markus, and their teammates are invited to one last adventure before heading home. This time, they're going on a treasure hunt in the heart of London. The coach has hidden clues around the city, and the boys must find them all to uncover the final treasure.

The first clue **was** hidden at the British Museum. "We **found** the first clue here," Lukas said as he picked up a small piece of paper. It **said**, "To find the next clue, go to the place where kings and queens are crowned."

"That's Westminster Abbey!" Markus **exclaimed**. "We've been there already, so we know the way!"

The boys hurried to Westminster Abbey, where they searched for the second clue. Markus **looked** near the statues, while Lukas **searched** by the tombs. Finally, one of their teammates **spotted** a small envelope hidden under a bench. Inside, the note **read**, "Your next clue is where time begins."

"The Royal Observatory!" Lukas said. "That's where the Prime Meridian is—it's the line that marks the start of time!"

Off they went to the Royal Observatory. When they arrived, they **looked** around the famous clock and **found** the third clue. This time, the note **said**, "To find the final treasure, go to the place where you learned how to play like champions."

"The football stadium!" Markus shouted. "That's where we played our final match!"

The team rushed to the stadium. When they arrived, they began searching everywhere: by the stands, near the field, and even in the locker rooms. Finally, Lukas **saw** a small box hidden under a seat in the stands. He opened it and inside **was** a trophy, with the words: "You are all champions."

The boys couldn't believe it. "We **did** it!" Lukas said, holding the trophy up high.

Their coach arrived with a big smile on his face. "You **worked** together to find all the clues, just like you played together on the field. This treasure hunt was a reminder that teamwork, both on and off the field, is what makes you champions."

Markus and Lukas smiled at each other. "This season **was** amazing," Markus said. "I'll never forget any of it."

Lukas nodded. "And I'll never forget that last clue. It led us to something even better than a treasure—it reminded us of how far we've come as a team."

Vocabulary (English - Deutsch)

English	Deutsch
treasure hunt	die Schatzsuche
clue	der Hinweis
crown	die Krone
stadium	das Stadion
observatory	das Observatorium
to find	finden
to search	suchen
to solve	lösen
trophy	die Trophäe
to crown	krönen

Gap Text: Simple Past

Complete the sentences with the correct form of the **Simple Past**:

1. Lukas ____ (to find) the first clue at the British Museum.
2. The boys ____ (to search) for the second clue at Westminster Abbey.

3. Markus ____ (to spot) the small envelope under the bench.
4. They ____ (to look) for the final treasure at the football stadium.
5. Lukas ____ (to see) the small box under a seat in the stands.

Answer the questions about the story

1. Where did the boys find the first clue?
2. What did the second clue tell them to do?
3. Where did they find the third clue?
4. What was the final treasure?
5. How did the boys feel after completing the treasure hunt?

Bring the words into the correct order

1. found / Lukas / clue / the / first.
2. searched / for / the / clue / second / they.
3. clue / told / second / them / the / what?
4. saw / the / under / Lukas / seat / a / small / box.
5. treasure / find / did / they / the / where?

Match the words with the correct translation

Words (English) Translations (Deutsch)

1. Treasure hunt A. die Schatzsuche

Words (English) Translations (Deutsch)

2. Clue	B. der Hinweis
3. Observatory	D. das Observatorium
4. Crown	C. die Krone
5. Trophy	E. die Trophäe

Quiz

1. Where did the boys find the second clue?
    - A) At the British Museum
    - B) At Westminster Abbey
    - C) At the Royal Observatory
2. What did the third clue tell them?
    - A) To go to the Royal Observatory
    - B) To go to the stadium
    - C) To go to a museum
3. Where was the final treasure hidden?
    - A) In the locker room
    - B) On the football field
    - C) Under a seat in the stands
4. What was the final treasure?
    - A) A trophy
    - B) A medal
    - C) A football

5. How did the coach describe the team after they completed the treasure hunt?
    - A) As hardworking players
    - B) As champions who work together
    - C) As strong individual players

Translation: DER LETZTE HINWEIS

Nach ihrer unglaublichen Saison und dem Sieg im letzten Spiel wurden Lukas, Markus und ihre Teamkollegen zu einem letzten Abenteuer eingeladen, bevor sie nach Hause zurückkehrten. Diesmal machten sie eine Schatzsuche im Herzen Londons. Der Trainer hatte Hinweise in der ganzen Stadt versteckt, und die Jungs mussten alle finden, um den letzten Schatz zu entdecken.

Der erste Hinweis **war** im British Museum versteckt. "Wir **haben** den ersten Hinweis hier gefunden", sagte Lukas, als er ein kleines Stück Papier aufhob. Darauf **stand**: "Um den nächsten Hinweis zu finden, gehe zu dem Ort, an dem Könige und Königinnen gekrönt werden."

"Das ist die Westminster Abbey!" **rief** Markus. "Wir waren schon dort, also kennen wir den Weg!"

Die Jungs eilten zur Westminster Abbey, wo sie nach dem zweiten Hinweis suchten. Markus **schaute** in der Nähe der Statuen, während Lukas bei den Gräbern **suchte**. Schließlich **entdeckte** einer ihrer Teamkollegen einen kleinen Umschlag, der unter einer

Bank versteckt war. Darin **stand**: "Euer nächster Hinweis ist dort, wo die Zeit beginnt."

"Das Royal Observatory!" sagte Lukas. "Dort ist der Nullmeridian – das ist die Linie, die den Beginn der Zeit markiert!"

Schnell gingen sie zum Royal Observatory. Als sie ankamen, **suchten** sie um die berühmte Uhr herum und **fanden** den dritten Hinweis. Diesmal **stand** auf dem Zettel: "Um den letzten Schatz zu finden, gehe zu dem Ort, an dem ihr gelernt habt, wie Champions zu spielen."

"Das Fußballstadion!" rief Markus. "Dort haben wir unser letztes Spiel gespielt!"

Das Team eilte zum Stadion. Dort angekommen, suchten sie überall: bei den Tribünen, in der Nähe des Spielfelds und sogar in den Umkleideräumen. Schließlich **sah** Lukas eine kleine Box, die unter einem Sitz in der Tribüne versteckt war. Er öffnete sie und darin **war** eine Trophäe mit den Worten: "Ihr seid alle Champions."

Die Jungs konnten es kaum glauben. "Wir **haben** es geschafft!" sagte Lukas und hielt die Trophäe hoch.

Ihr Trainer kam mit einem breiten Lächeln auf sie zu. "Ihr **habt** zusammengearbeitet, um alle Hinweise zu finden, genau wie ihr auf dem Spielfeld zusammen gespielt habt. Diese Schatzsuche sollte euch daran erinnern, dass Teamarbeit, sowohl auf als auch neben dem Spielfeld, euch zu Champions macht."

Markus und Lukas lächelten sich an. "Diese Saison **war** unglaublich", sagte Markus. "Ich werde keinen Moment davon vergessen."

Lukas nickte. "Und ich werde diesen letzten Hinweis nie vergessen. Er hat uns zu etwas noch Besserem als einem Schatz geführt – er hat uns daran erinnert, wie weit wir als Team gekommen sind."

➢ Answers

Gap Text:

1. found
2. searched
3. spotted
4. looked
5. saw

Answer the questions about the story

1. At the British Museum
2. It told them to go to Westminster Abbey.
3. At the Royal Observatory
4. A trophy with the words: "You are all champions."
5. They felt proud and excited after completing the treasure hunt.

Bring the words into the correct order

1. Lukas found the first clue.
2. They searched for the second clue.

3. What did the second clue tell them?
4. Lukas saw a small box under a seat.
5. Where did they find the treasure?

Match the words with the correct translation

1. A | 2. B | 3. D | 4. C | 5. E

Quiz

1. B) At Westminster Abbey
2. A) To go to the Royal Observatory
3. C) Under a seat in the stands
4. A) A trophy
5. B) As champions who work together

12 | THE SURPRISE GUEST – Present Continuous

Lukas and Markus are in the middle of a special football practice. Their coach has arranged a surprise for the team, but he hasn't told them what it is yet. The boys are all warming up on the field, talking about what the surprise could be.

"What do you think it is?" Lukas asks Markus while stretching his legs.

"I'm not sure," Markus replies, "but I think it's going to be something really exciting!"

Suddenly, they hear a loud cheer coming from the stands. The boys stop what they're doing and look up. To their amazement, they see a famous football player walking onto the field!

"Is that...?" Lukas starts to ask, his eyes wide with disbelief.

"Yes, it's him!" Markus shouts, jumping up and down. "It's the famous player from our favorite team!"

The coach gathers the team together and announces, "Today, you're all going to learn from one of the best players in the world. He's going to teach you some advanced skills and play a match with you!"

The boys can't believe it. They're standing in front of their football hero, and he's about to play with them!

As the practice begins, the famous player is showing them how to dribble faster and pass more accurately. Lukas and Markus are focused, trying to learn as much as they can.

"Are we really playing with him?" Lukas whispers to Markus, still in awe.

"Yes, and we're getting better because of it!" Markus grins.

By the end of the day, the boys have learned many new techniques, and they feel inspired by their surprise guest. "This is the best practice ever," Lukas says as they walk off the field.

Markus nods. "I can't wait to try these new skills in our next match!"

Vocabulary (English - Deutsch)

English	Deutsch
guest	der Gast
surprise	die Überraschung

English	Deutsch
famous	berühmt
practice	das Training
dribblc	dribbeln
to learn	lernen
to cheer	jubeln
technique	die Technik
advanced	fortgeschritten

Gap Text: Present Continuous

Complete the sentences with the correct form of the Present Continuous:

1. The boys _____ (to warm) up on the field.
2. Markus _____ (to talk) to Lukas about the surprise.
3. They _____ (to learn) from a famous football player.
4. Lukas _____ (to try) to dribble faster.
5. Markus _____ (to practice) his passes.

Answer the questions about the story

1. What are the boys doing at the beginning of the story?
2. Who is the surprise guest at the football practice?
3. What skills does the famous player teach the boys?
4. How do Lukas and Markus feel about the surprise?
5. What are the boys planning to do with their new skills?

Bring the words into the correct order

1. guest / is / famous / a / the / there.
2. are / new / the / skills / learning / boys.
3. Lukas / is / dribbling / faster.
4. excited / are / the / boys / very.
5. showing / them / techniques / player / is / the / advanced.

Match the words with the correct translation

Words (English)	Translations (Deutsch)
1. Surprise	A. die Überraschung
2. Guest	C. der Gast
3. Practice	E. das Training
4. Learn	B. lernen
5. Famous	D. berühmt

Quiz

1. What are the boys learning at the football practice?
    - A) Running faster
    - B) Advanced football skills
    - C) How to be a coach
2. Who is the special guest at the practice?
    - A) A coach
    - B) A famous football player

- C) The boys' parents

3. What are Lukas and Markus feeling during the practice?
   - A) Bored
   - B) Excited
   - C) Nervous
4. What does the guest player teach the boys?
   - A) How to run longer distances
   - B) How to dribble and pass better
   - C) How to score goals
5. What do the boys plan to do with their new skills?
   - A) Use them in their next match
   - B) Show them off to their friends
   - C) Teach their coach

Translation: Der Überraschungsgast

Lukas und Markus sind mitten in einem besonderen Fußballtraining. Ihr Trainer hat eine Überraschung für die Mannschaft vorbereitet, aber er hat ihnen noch nicht verraten, was es ist. Die Jungen wärmen sich auf dem Spielfeld auf und reden darüber, was die Überraschung sein könnte.

„Was glaubst du, was es ist?" fragt Lukas, während er seine Beine dehnt.

„Ich weiß es nicht," antwortet Markus, „aber ich denke, es wird etwas wirklich Spannendes sein!"

Plötzlich hören sie ein lautes Jubeln von den Zuschauerrängen. Die Jungen halten inne und schauen hinauf. Zu ihrem Erstaunen sehen sie einen berühmten Fußballspieler, der auf das Spielfeld kommt!

„Ist das…?“ beginnt Lukas zu fragen, seine Augen weit vor Unglauben.

„Ja, das ist er!“ ruft Markus und springt auf und ab. „Es ist der berühmte Spieler aus unserer Lieblingsmannschaft!“

Der Trainer versammelt die Mannschaft und verkündet: „Heute werdet ihr von einem der besten Spieler der Welt lernen. Er wird euch einige fortgeschrittene Fähigkeiten beibringen und ein Spiel mit euch spielen!“

Die Jungen können es kaum glauben. Sie stehen vor ihrem Fußballidol, und er wird gleich mit ihnen spielen!

Während des Trainings zeigt der berühmte Spieler ihnen, wie sie schneller dribbeln und genauer passen können. Lukas und Markus konzentrieren sich und versuchen, so viel wie möglich zu lernen.

„Spielen wir wirklich mit ihm?“ flüstert Lukas Markus zu, immer noch voller Ehrfurcht.

„Ja, und wir werden dadurch besser!“ grinst Markus.

Am Ende des Tages haben die Jungen viele neue Techniken gelernt und fühlen sich von ihrem Überraschungsgast inspiriert. „Das war das beste Training überhaupt,“ sagt Lukas, als sie das Spielfeld verlassen.

Markus nickt. „Ich kann es kaum erwarten, diese neuen Fähigkeiten in unserem nächsten Spiel auszuprobieren!“

Answers

Gap Text: Present Continuous

1. are warming
2. is talking
3. are learning
4. is trying
5. is practicing

Answer the questions about the story

1. They are warming up and talking about the surprise.
2. A famous football player is the surprise guest.
3. The famous player teaches them how to dribble faster and pass more accurately.
4. Lukas and Markus are excited and thrilled by the surprise.
5. They plan to use their new skills in the next match.

Bring the words into the correct order

1. There is a famous guest.
2. The boys are learning new skills.
3. Lukas is dribbling faster.
4. The boys are very excited.
5. The player is showing them advanced techniques.

Match the words with the correct translation

1. A | 2. C | 3. E | 4. B | 5. D

Quiz

1. B) Advanced football skills
2. B) A famous football player
3. B) Excited
4. B) How to dribble and pass better
5. A) Use them in their next match

13 | THE UNEXPECTED RAIN – Future Simple

One afternoon, Lukas and Markus are getting ready to play a match with their team. The weather forecast says it might rain, but the sky is still clear.

“We’ll probably be fine,” Lukas says confidently.

Markus, however, looks a little worried. “I don’t know... What if it starts raining in the middle of the match?”

Just as they are about to begin, dark clouds appear overhead. The coach looks up and announces, “It will rain soon. We need to decide if we’ll continue playing or wait.”

"I think we'll get wet, but it won't stop us!" Markus says with a smile.

The match begins, and sure enough, the rain starts falling just a few minutes later. At first, it's just a drizzle, but soon it becomes heavier. The boys keep playing, splashing through puddles as they run.

"We'll win this game, rain or shine!" Lukas shouts to his teammates.

Even though the field is muddy and slippery, the boys are determined to finish the game. By the time the final whistle blows, they are soaked but happy—they've won the match despite the weather.

Afterward, as they head back to the locker room, the coach says, "You'll remember this day for a long time. Not every team plays this well in the rain!"

Vocabulary (English - Deutsch)

English	Deutsch
weather	das Wetter
forecast	die Wettervorhersage
drizzle	der Nieselregen
puddle	die Pfütze
to decide	entscheiden
to get wet	nass werden

English	Deutsch
slippery	rutschig
to win	gewinnen
whistle	die Pfeife

Gap Text: Future Simple

Complete the sentences with the correct form of the Future Simple:

1. Lukas _____ (to play) in the match even if it rains.
2. The coach thinks it _____ (to rain) soon.
3. Markus _____ (to score) a goal, no matter the weather.
4. They _____ (to remember) this day for a long time.
5. The team _____ (to win) the match despite the rain.

Answer the questions about the story

1. What does the weather forecast say?
2. What happens just before the match starts?
3. How do Lukas and Markus react to the rain?
4. How does the weather affect the game?
5. What does the coach say after the match?

Bring the words into the correct order

1. will / rain / it / soon.
2. match / play / will / the / they.
3. win / the / will / match / team / the.

4. wet / we / will / get.
5. puddles / running / are / through / they.

Match the words with the correct translation

Words (English)	Translations (Deutsch)
1. Rain	A. der Regen
2. Puddle	C. die Pfütze
3. Weather	E. das Wetter
4. Whistle	B. die Pfeife
5. Slippery	D. rutschig

Quiz

1. What is the weather forecast for the day?
    - A) Clear skies
    - B) Rain
    - C) Snow
2. How do Lukas and Markus feel about playing in the rain?
    - A) Nervous
    - B) Excited
    - C) Scared
3. What happens during the match?
    - A) The rain stops
    - B) The rain gets heavier
    - C) It starts snowing

4. How does the rain affect the game?
   - A) The boys keep playing and win
   - B) The game is cancelled
   - C) The match is delayed
5. What does the coach say at the end of the match?
   - A) "You'll remember this day."
   - B) "You need more practice."
   - C) "The weather wasn't a problem."

Translation: Der unerwartete Regen

Eines Nachmittags bereiten sich Lukas und Markus darauf vor, mit ihrer Mannschaft ein Spiel zu spielen. Die Wettervorhersage sagt, dass es regnen könnte, aber der Himmel ist noch klar.

„Es wird wahrscheinlich gut gehen," sagt Lukas selbstbewusst.

Markus sieht jedoch etwas besorgt aus. „Ich weiß nicht... Was, wenn es mitten im Spiel anfängt zu regnen?"

Gerade als sie anfangen wollen, ziehen dunkle Wolken über ihnen auf. Der Trainer schaut nach oben und verkündet: „Es wird bald regnen. Wir müssen entscheiden, ob wir weiterspielen oder warten."

„Ich denke, wir werden nass, aber das wird uns nicht aufhalten!" sagt Markus mit einem Lächeln.

Das Spiel beginnt, und schon nach ein paar Minuten fängt es an zu regnen. Zuerst ist es nur ein Nieselregen, aber bald wird es stärker.

Die Jungen spielen weiter und laufen durch die Pfützen, während sie rennen.

„Wir werden dieses Spiel gewinnen, ob es regnet oder nicht!“ ruft Lukas seinen Teamkollegen zu.

Auch wenn das Spielfeld matschig und rutschig ist, sind die Jungen entschlossen, das Spiel zu Ende zu spielen. Als der Schlusspfiff ertönt, sind sie völlig durchnässt, aber glücklich – sie haben das Spiel trotz des Wetters gewonnen.

Auf dem Weg zurück in die Umkleidekabine sagt der Trainer: „Ihr werdet euch noch lange an diesen Tag erinnern. Nicht jede Mannschaft spielt so gut im Regen!“

➢ Answers

Gap Text: Future Simple

1. will play
2. will rain
3. will score
4. will remember
5. will win

Answer the questions about the story

1. The weather forecast says it might rain.
2. Dark clouds appear, and the coach says it will rain soon.
3. They are optimistic and keep playing even in the rain.
4. The field becomes slippery, but the boys keep playing and win the game.

5. The coach says they will remember this day for a long time.

Bring the words into the correct order

1. It will rain soon.
2. They will play the match.
3. The team will win the match.
4. We will get wet.
5. They are running through puddles.

Match the words with the correct translation

1. A | 2. C | 3. E | 4. B | 5. D

Quiz

1. B) Rain
2. B) Excited
3. B) The rain gets heavier
4. A) The boys keep playing and win
5. A) "You'll remember this day

SCAN ME

Printed in Poland
by Amazon Fulfillment
Poland Sp. z o.o., Wrocław

54461703R00059